PETUNIA WOLF

THE CASE CRACKER

BOOK 1

WRITTEN AND ILLUSTRATED BY

AFSHEEN SHEIKH

Young Author Academy
BECOME A PUBLISHED AUTHOR

Thanks a trillion to my wonderful parents
for motivating me to reach my goals
and achieve my dreams.

Words can't describe how grateful I am.

Thanks a million Ms. Annemieke for
making this possible!

Thanks a lot to all my well-wishers, teachers,
family members, and friends!

Contents

PETUNIA WOLF AND THE CITY OF EUTOPIA   P47

PETUNIA WOLF AND THE CASE OF
THE MISSING PRINCESS   P71

Dear kids,

I have just returned from Arabia after solving a flummoxed case.

This book you'll be reading now is amazeballs and marvellous and it contains three bewildering and cool cases.

They were full of twists and turns. I had to solve two cases on vacation, can you believe it? Yet, solving cases is my specialty, so I don't have any problem.

Read more to find out more....

Petunia

WHO IS PETUNIA WOLF?

Petunia Wolf is an awesome thirty year-old woman. She is a detective and an undercover agent of The Police of Furors.

Petunia is kind-hearted and daring and she has pretty green eyes, bright skin colour and beautiful short hair.

She is also very slim and lovely.

Petunia is the No. 1 detective in the city of Furors which is a city in Masikundra. She is very famous for her wonderful work there.

She believes,

"Get your fears away and reach greater heights!"

Petunia Wolf

and

Vacation Time

- Chapter One -

Vacation Location

"Yay! It's finally vacation. I can't wait to go to the City of Ruins. I think it is historical. Take out the caravan, Milly!" Petunia said to her best friend and roommate, Milly. She was super excited.

They opened the GPS system and searched for the location of the City of Ruins. Milly assumed that it would take at least nine hours to reach there by road.

Petunia replied, "Absolutely fine with me. Milly, if it is okay for you, then we will get started."

Milly agreed and they set off. The journey was so quiet and boring. Petunia tried reading a magazine and playing a game on the phone. However, soon, she got too sleepy and fell asleep.

When Petunia woke, they had already reached their destination. The duo was horrified when they saw the sign board that read, "The City of Ruins," because it was covered with dirty, red hand prints. They slowly and cautiously entered the city, unsure of what they would see.

She became terrified when she saw the condition of the people. They looked like zombies and outside every house, there was a fire burning trash. It was so stinky and gross. They became frightened and rushed to their hotel room, which was not too far away.

Their hotel room was not at all appealing. Inside the hotel room, the wallpaper was peeling off and cracked, and the bed stood on rocks. It was made of hard stones. It did not even look sleep-worthy.

Petunia gauged, "Oh my god! This city is not at all a historical site. I feel that it should be renamed "The Worst Scary City." Milly seconded her.

They were not happy with their decision to travel there, particularly as they had booked a trip to explore the city for two months.

The girls looked out of the window and noticed something weird. The sun was not even setting, despite it being twelve in the morning. What a shocking surprise! They spent some time chatting together and then went to sleep somehow.

Petunia had a nightmare and woke up screaming with beads of sweat on her forehead. She dreamt that she was being eaten by the people of the city. In her dream, she was tied up and was getting grilled like a chicken on a barbecue stick. She could not sleep at all after that.

The next day, Petunia became sick due to food poisoning. It was oyster-rot that was served for dinner.

Obviously, no-one cared about her except for Milly. She had vomited several times and had a high fever. Milly decided to go to the store to buy medicine for her.

When she reached the store, it looked as if it was a hundred years old.

It had insects crawling along the floor and there was a strong odour of rotten meat and fruits in the air. Eww! She closed her nose with her fingers and managed to find the medicine which was safe and NOT expired.

She went back to the room and gave Petunia the medicine. She eventually told her all about the store and how disturbing it was. Petunia thanked her for finding her some medicine. After four to five hours, she felt much better.

They decided to go out for a walk to get some fresh air. Suddenly, they saw a guy chasing a girl around with a knife.

Both of them immediately sprinted to the spot to help the girl and Petunia asserted, "Hey! Why are you chasing that girl with a knife? Don't you even have any mercy? She is just a child."

The man retorted, "She was stealing food from my hotel room."

They stared seriously at him as if they were going to kill him; he just became more furious and ran away.

They asked the girl if she was safe. Then they took her to their room and had a polite conversation with her.

The girl mumbled, "My name is Diana. I am a citizen of this place. I do not have parents. I am just scared to even live here."

Petunia announced, "Diana, don't you panic. I will adopt you and you can be my daughter from now on. I will take care of you and always protect you, but why were you stealing food?"

Diana explained, "Since no one cares about me here, I am forced to do so. If I don't steal food, I will die of hunger."

Petunia forgave her as it was necessary for her survival. Diana felt blessed and hugged Petunia. She called her Mamma.

They would walk together, play, draw and take funny selfies. Petunia and Milly even made her a swing. They were extremely delighted to have such a courteous girl. It was like having a new life with her. They spent their whole day with her.

Petunia decided that she would take her home and provide her with a high quality of education when they returned from their trip. Diana started living a peaceful and merry life with her new mom. Both of them, each took turns to spend time with Diana in their hotel room. They were all happy.

Ten crazy days passed by so quickly!

- Chapter Two -

A New Friend

It was the eleventh day into Petunia's vacation. She, Milly and Diana decided to go out for a walk. The weather was pleasant, however, they wore masks because the smell was too bad.

Just then, they saw a poor lady sitting on the roadside. She just had a box to live in and a piece of cardboard in her hand that read, 'Help Please.'

No one cared at all.

Petunia approached her, had a discussion and then took her to the hotel room as a friend. Now, they were all a little squeezed up in their room, but they managed.

The lady told Petunia that her name was Lydia and that she was homeless. Petunia thought for a while and then decided to make her a 3-D printed house.

She called the 3-D printing Department of Furors and ordered the construction of the house.

The builders came the next day and got to work. They installed some pretty furniture and made the small house look as beautiful as the interior of a mansion.

Lydia loved her new home and expressed her gratitude. She insisted that they stay with her in the new house as she already knew the status of the hotel room. They agreed and were super-duper jolly.

She was very kind to them and offered yummy food and drinks. She would give Diana cookies and milkshakes. Petunia's vacation experience was much better now! Yahoo!

They even wrote a poem together about 'Friends'-

Friends are awesome,

Just like blossoms.

They make us feel comfortable,

Our friendship is unbreakable.

Without them, we feel so bored,

They never make us feel ignored.

Nobody can have fun without them.

They had a lot of fun but soon Lydia's dark secrets started to be revealed. What Diana, Petunia and Milly did not know was that she worked for a big gang and she had a rare disease which made her sick very suddenly, yet they took great care of her.

After some investigation, the girls discovered that she was associated with a group of unsavoury people, in a gang.

Petunia didn't have a good feeling thinking about who Lydia was working for and she made up her mind to further investigate and nab the gang before they caused any trouble to herself, Diana or Milly.

- Chapter Three -

A Huge Problem

Another two days passed and Petunia had forgotten about the gang. She, Milly, Diana and Lydia were having a stroll in the park after eating their breakfast. They had cheese balls and chicken pasta made by Lydia. They were walking like angels with no duties.

Suddenly, Petunia felt some sort of discomfort and became unconscious. After an hour or so, she opened her eyes slowly. When she tried moving her hands, feet and wanted to talk, she couldn't.

To her dismay, she realized that she had been kidnapped. She saw the room in which she was locked in. It was dark and creepy.

She then heard a familiar voice and noticed that someone was coming towards her. In an instant, she realized that it was Lydia's voice.

She thought that Lydia had possibly also been kidnapped and was trying to ask for help, but then Lydia came nearer and started to chuckle.

She spoke, "Hey Petunia! Thanks for your help, but do you know who I actually am? I am the secretary of the man who was trying to kill Diana, and he is the leader of the Wing Gang. He is out of the city and has commanded me to kidnap you and your dumb little friends."

Lydia pulled the tape off Petunia's face. Petunia panted and said, "You will never get away with this! I am the No. 1 detective within Furors and you will be captured and thrown into jail."

"Go away you fraud!" she grinned and left her with the door tightly shut.

Petunia always had emergency tools in her pockets, so she carefully grabbed a blade and cut the tape with it. She was now free. She slowly opened the door and searched for Milly and Diana.

She saw Lydia misbehaving with Diana and also threatening her. She fumed like a volcano, took an injection from her tool kit and ran towards Lydia. She injected Lydia to render her unconscious and subsequently freed Diana.

Diana let on that she overheard a phone conversation that Lydia had sent Milly to the City of Kelly.

Petunia thought, 'Oh, sounds like another horrifying city.'

- Chapter Four -

The City of Kelly

Petunia and Diana managed to escape from being held captive and rushed to their hotel room. They searched for the City of Kelly on her map. Once she found it, she set off with Diana in Milly's camper. She drove for two hours continuously when finally, they reached the City of Kelly.

Just like the City of Ruins, the scene was terrible. There were people running after each other with daggers, gigantic swords and sticks of fire.

The place was also very dirty. It should have been called, 'The City of Killer Skunks.'

Petunia closed her nose and entered quietly so that nobody would notice. Diana imitated her mom.

After a while, they saw Milly running wildly and crazily. She even had one white eye.

Petunia was startled and ran right towards her. She asked, "Milly, is that really you? What happened to you?" Milly babbled like a small baby.

Suddenly, Petunia received a call from an unknown number. She picked it up and a man started talking on the other end. "Hello to you! I am the leader of Wing Gang. This is my town and I think you see Milly on the road. Well, she isn't real at all. She's just a robot. Milly's with me. Give me fifteen million dollars for her release."

Petunia bravely responded, "How come you know? Do you have some spies around here of yours? Ok! Collect the money. Inform me where to come right now!" The man laughed devilishly and mentioned, "There are three clues in this whole city. Solve them and they will help you to reach my house. Remember to keep the money ready, if not, I will make your daughter and your bestie suffer for sure. Good luck….

THE FIRST CLUE IS:-
DURING THE NIGHT
HELPER OF SAILORS
HAS A BRIGHT LIGHT.

"Ok, bye for now miss!"

Petunia angrily kept the phone in her pocket. She suddenly had a stupendous idea.

Let us see what she does next......

- Chapter Five -

Finding Clues

She knew about which place the man was talking about. It was clearly the light house. She reached there with her daughter.

It was dark inside but they had torch lights with them. The only thing that was unusual in the lighthouse was that there were tons of books.

She touched one of the books and a huge tunnel suddenly opened up. It had a bloody stairway inside. She and Diana went into it without any fear but what they saw at the end of the staircase was horrendous.

It was an obstacle course and not just any obstacle course; the ones that sometimes lead to severe injuries and even death!

Diana shrieked so loud that the birds above the lighthouse flew away in fright. Petunia calmed her down and told Diana to stay back. Petunia slowly and cautiously went through all the obstacles and helped Diana pass too.

Petunia just realized that there was a cut on her arm from a knife, so she tied a piece of cloth onto the injury and moved on.

There was a scintillating golden box in front of her. She opened it and saw a piece of paper inside. It contained a clue.

It read,

Petunia thought about it and instantaneously got it. It was the park. Now, the only thing she was worried was about the size of the park, it was very big.

The park was two kilometers away, so she and Diana walked all the way there. There was a map of the park at the entrance. She studied it carefully and noticed a place that had no name.

She pondered, thinking that must be where the 3rd clue could be. She rushed to the location with her daughter and explored all around the place. They found a microscopic silver box in that area.

Petunia opened it and was astounded to see the picture of a gigantic mansion.

On the back of the photo, was written~

CONGRATS PETUNIA!
YOU HAVE FOUND THE LAST CLUE.

THIS PICTURE IS MY HOME.

COME AND GET MILLY IF YOU CAN.

- Chapter Six-

Problem Solved or Not?

With a mind blowing plot in her mind, Petunia called The Police of Furors and informed them of her strategy to get Milly back safe and sound. She even told them to arrest Lydia. She sent them a message sharing with them, her live location.

Petunia decided to go to the man's house with Diana. She reached there in no time and discovered that he was not there. The main door was left wide open. She squealed Milly's name at least five times.

After a while, she heard feeble cries. It was Milly's voice.

Petunia searched all of the rooms and at last, she found Milly locked in a cupboard with just one tiny breathing hole. She immediately took her out but then the leader arrived home. He was tall and skinny.

He came to Petunia and applauded, "Oh great! You have reached my home. Name's Sebastian. Nice job."

Petunia avowed, "I don't say thanks to criminals."

In the spur of the moment, an immensely large net dropped down and trapped Petunia. The net was enclosed in a jumbo ball-like structure.

Sebastian smirked and boasted, "Well! How did you like my style of capturing you, Miss?"

Petunia kept quiet and thought, 'That's all? What else would he do? He's just trying to put the wind up me.'

The ball started to lift and rise swiftly through the air. It came down and was thrown side-wards like a slingshot. Petunia grappled to get out of the net.

She tried to do all kinds of things to get out, but with no success.

Abruptly, they all heard police sirens coming closer. Sebastian became petrified and attempted to escape but out of nowhere, came Diana and hit him with a large rod. He collapsed. The police came and arrested him. Diana teased him mocking, "Busted! Ha-ha!!!"

The police released Petunia from the ball using a remote in Sebastian's pocket. Petunia thanked them and especially the little hero, Diana.

They congratulated both Petunia and Diana for their intelligence and audacity.

There were two police cars outside the mansion. One car took him to prison. Petunia was given the first aid in another car. A policeman informed her that they had arrested Lydia. She sighed a huge sigh of relief.

Once the first car reached Furors police station and Petunia's wounds were treated, they arranged a video call and requested her to check whether the lady that they arrested was Lydia.

Petunia wailed. "No! Oh no!" in a perturbed voice. She screamed that they had arrested the wrong Lydia!

- Chapter Seven -

Attempt to Arrest Lydia

Petunia requested that Milly and Diana go to live in the 3D printed house until she returned. Then she started working with the police to investigate the possible capture of the right Lydia. She asked them to find out the most common criminal escape routes. The police notified her about three such routes. One led to The City of Ruins, the other led to the City of Lisa and the last one, to the City of Eutopia.

Petunia sat nearby and researched those particular cities using her smartphone. The worst of them was the City of Lisa, so she decided to go there first.

Petunia analyzed a lot of the data and information and came to the conclusion that, the City of Ruins could not be where Lydia had escaped, because she already knew that they had been there.

The City of Lisa could be where she had escaped, because that's the place with lowest security and the city had zero police stations.

The City of Eutopia could not be where she escaped, as it was a place with very high security with many police stations.

Petunia and the police proceeded to the city in disguise. They found a somewhat weird hotel where Lydia could probably stay in.

They inquired at the reception about the recent bookings in the hotel. The receptionist informed them that a woman named Ayumi Lydia had booked a room there. Petunia grinned and barged into her room. Yes! Yes! Yes! There was Ms. Lydia.

Lydia ran out of the window swiftly. She had a rope tied to the window to escape if any problem as such occurred.

"Well planned Lydia! I will surely catch you," exclaimed Petunia. She followed Lydia rapidly. Lydia was a very fast runner and she got away! Petunia ran back to the hotel room and told the police to contact all of the police stations in nearby cities to tell them about the new~Most Wanted Criminal~ Ayumi Lydia.

The police did so but no-one picked up the call, except for the one police station, Eutopia Police from the City of Eutopia.

Petunia talked to them and informed them about the whole incident. The Furors' Police and the Eutopia Police decided to team up to solve this rather mysterious case.

- Chapter Eight -

Solving Lydia's Case... Not Easy!

After a few hours, the
Police of Eutopia
reached there. The
team searched for clues
from her hotel room.
Woohoo! they found
one! It was a

photograph of her standing near a sign board
reading, 'City of Leonia.'

Petunia found the location and took the police to
examine further. There, she saw a hefty man with
a sword in his hand stopping them from entering
the city.

The man looked like some sort of caveman. He
wore a garment made of animal skin.

Petunia questioned the man but he didn't reply. It was as if he didn't understand anything.

Suddenly, all the policemen fainted and fell onto the ground. Petunia was shocked and rushed them to a nearby hospital. All of them were taken inside. Petunia sat, worried on a chair.

After sometime, a doctor arrived to give them check-ups and told her that they all were fine. There was medicine in their water, which ultimately rendered them unconscious. He told them that they needed two days rest. Petunia was determined to solve this case within these two days. She went back to the hefty man and this time she was carrying a huge sword.

Petunia tried to talk to him, but no response again. Instead, he started hitting her and a prolonged fight broke out between them.

Luckily, Petunia didn't get hurt too badly. That man, however, got hurt badly and fell onto the ground making a frightful sound.

Petunia noticed that something fell from his pocket. It looked like an ID of some sort. She quickly picked it up and ran inside the city.

She sat peacefully and started looking at the ID card. It read,

DAVID DARINGTON

LDIAY GNAG

GGAN LEADRE-AYMUI LDIAY

oN. FO POEPEL-2

There was just one problem. All of the words except the first line were jumbled. Petunia started to unjumble them and the results were indeed very horrifying,

DAVID DARINGTON

LYDIA GANG

GANG LEADER-AYUMI LYDIA

No. OF PEOPLE-2

Lydia had a gang on her own! The man and Lydia were clearly partners.

As soon as she figured it, out of the blue, someone from behind hit her head really hard. Her head was slightly bleeding and as a result, she fell to the ground, senseless.

- Chapter Nine -

Kidnapped Again

Petunia woke up after a while and found herself in a room in an abandoned house. Lydia and David were standing there, staring at her.

"Hey! Liked my awesome comeback. Try to arrest me if you can. Ha-ha! You can't do it!" Lydia sniggered.

Lydia and David ran out of there and locked the front door of the house! Petunia was locked inside.

She had no signal on her phone and the battery was almost dead. Surprisingly, there was a knock on the door. Petunia quickly tried to reach for the scissors on the nearby table to tear the tight rope around her.

Slowly and carefully, she tore the rope. It took her ten minutes to do so. At last, yay! She was free. She went to the front of the room and noticed flames outside. Wait what! Fire!? Lydia and David had set the building on fire and left her to die!

Petunia got some water from a room, slowly opened the windows one by one and doused off the flames. In that moment, it was like Petunia's job evolved from a detective to a fire fighter. She was fortunate to have enough water to put out the fire. From all the exertion, she was exhausted and sat on the floor to relax for a bit.

She tried to escape from the windows, but all of them were too small for her to climb through. After three hours of attempting to break the door, there was a knock. Petunia went to check who it was. This time, it was Officer Shawn from the Furors Police! He was from Poland and spoke Esperanto. He was also very daring and bold.

Again, Petunia attempted to open the door but she forgot that it was locked. She shouted to the officer, "Officer! I am stuck here. This is Petunia Wolf. Get me out of here!"

The Officer heard her voice and quickly broke the door. He rescued her and took her to the clinic for the treatment of minor wounds on her hands and legs.

Petunia then narrated the whole incident and proclaimed, "Officer, call all other policemen! Let's solve this case." The officer called them all and they reported there in no time.

They dispersed around to locate the culprits but by this time, they were nowhere to be found.

Petunia asked them to search as far and wide as they could, as time had passed where they could now be anywhere.

The police searched around again and found one very stinky place, the trash bin area. Petunia approached the location with Officer Shawn to scrutinise the scene.

She opened one of the trash bins and was surprised to see it empty. Suspicious, once she touched inside the bin, a code machine automatically raised from within and asked her for a code. Petunia was sure now that something was fishy.

She entered random codes with different variations but none worked. She thought of the easiest code to try with, 123456789. She entered it and yes, it worked!

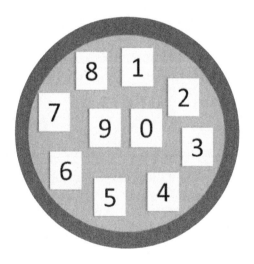

A mysterious tunnel opened there right in front of them and they both cautiously walked on in.

Petunia and the officer were astonished to see many things lying around. They spotted a picture of Lydia on the wall.

It looked like Lydia and David had their own secret hideout and as they went deeper, she just realized how strong her mini gang really was.

They found some of the most expensive gold and diamond items which were probably stolen by them. Petunia recollected seeing an article about these items in the newspaper about four to five months back.

She handed it over to officer Shawn for further exploration and needful action.

The tunnel was really deep. It had a dozen or so rooms. Evidently, Lydia and David were hiding somewhere there! They had to be. They called the whole police team in and the search began...

They found Lydia hiding in a corner, but when they moved closer, they realized that it was just a doll.

"Ugh!" screamed Petunia!

Alas, with a huge team of trained professionals, it still wasn't easy to catch them.

They were just too sly and smart to be caught.

- Chapter Ten -

Catching Ms. Sneaky at Last

Petunia and the Police decided to leave the underground hideout and retreat from the tunnel and return after some time.

After an hour, Petunia quietly snuck back in once more. She decided to look around some more, just in case they had relaxed and came out of hiding. She found both of them lying on a couch in the farthest room from the entrance.

She thought, 'How crazy of them? They are criminals and instead of escaping, they are relaxing. Seriously?'

She slowly came up behind them without being noticed and grabbed Lydia, but David escaped.

He could not escape.

A group of policemen were standing outside waiting to arrest him. They took both of them into custody. Petunia told the duo, "Try to get out of jail if you can. Ha-ha! You can't do it!" The police took them all to Eutopia Jail.

All the criminals were securely in jail now!

Petunia received a medal from the police for her extraordinary bravery. They were very happy with her gallant efforts.

She packed her things to return to the City of Ruins to see Diana and Milly. She decided to take them to another better place, the City of Eutopia.

Did you figure out the clue?

Lydia had a disease that made her sick

very suddenly. That's the reason she

was lying on the sofa.

Petunia Wolf

and

The City of Eutopia

- Chapter One -

Trip to the City of Eutopia

Petunia returned to Milly and Diana. They were glad to see her back. They hugged each other tightly and had a cool long chat. They realized that it had been just one month and Petunia had another whole month left.

They headed to the nearest and safest place, the City of Eutopia in Milly's camper. By their calculations, the trip was to take five hours. They stopped at Tipsy-Turban restaurant to enjoy some lunch along the way.

Petunia, Milly and Diana were delighted to eat some yummy food and be together after such a long time apart.

As they entered the city, they were fascinated with what they saw. The city was so pretty with fresh air and happy people walking around looking at so many attractions.

The first thing she did was book a luxurious hotel room for her and her friends. Then, she relaxed and took a nap for two hours while Milly and Diana played in the pool.

They enjoyed their stay there and had a lot of fun. Ten days elapsed. On the eleventh day, Petunia got a phone call from the police of Eutopia asking help to solve a puzzled case as they were so impressed when working with her in the earlier case.

Petunia consented, "Always at your service sir."

The police gave her all the details. "A psychopath is sending scary photographs of ghosts to people all around the city, demanding a million dollars.

If they denied, he would threaten to change their faces to ghosts and clowns with his invention.

A courageous person reported this to the police. "We have kept that person under high security for now to keep him safe."

Brave and brainy Petunia, began the process. First, she gathered details of people with psychiatric disorders there from the 'Special City Hospital.'

She made a list of seven such people,

1. Liam
2. Rio
3. Theo
4. Iggy
5. Edwin
6. Ace
7. Tool

The person who provided this information to her also informed her that three of them had recently escaped from the hospital- Iggy, Theo and Ace.

To Petunia, these three people were automatically made the prime suspects and she requested a search for them all around the city. She got hold of some people with psychiatric disorders and started her interrogation process.

- Chapter Two -

A Conversation

During the investigation, she found that none of the people that she was questioning had the qualities matching to the suspects. She let them go and continued her search for the dangerous trio.

On her way, she suddenly heard a sound from a sewer, beneath the ground. It was like a chorused ghost-sound. Petunia called upon some people to lift the sewer lid. She took a ladder and climbed in.

She found two people inside just sitting, kind of like ghouls. They started to walk towards her. Petunia fearlessly gave them a few punches and forced them sit. She was not afraid at all.

One of the strange characters made a sound of electricity crackling. It was then, that she realized that they were in fact, robots.

"Huh? These days all these criminals are using technology. I have to be careful!" ascertained Petunia.

She climbed out from the sewerage tunnels and brainstormed her next moves, when her phone suddenly rang. She was receiving a video call from a mysterious number. She answered the call and saw a man wearing a mask...

PETUNIA-   HELLO! YES, WHO IS THIS SPEAKING?

STRANGER-

HELLO! I AM
SILLY.
SEE THIS
PHOTOGRAPH.

PETUNIA-   PHOO! WHAT IS THAT?

STRANGER-   IT'S THE FACE OF A MAN I'VE SHOT
WITH MY GHOST BLASTER MACHINE
WHICH MAKES ONE LOOK LIKE A GHOST
OR A CREEPY CLOWN. I WAS HOPING TO
DO THE SAME THING TO YOU.

PETUNIA-   DO YOU EVEN KNOW WHO I AM?

STRANGER-   YES, I DO. YOU'RE PETUNIA WOLF.

             WHO DOESN'T KNOW?

PETUNIA-   DID YOU FIND ONLY ME TO TROUBLE?

             DON'T YOU KNOW I AM WORKING ON YOUR

             CASE? I CAN EASILY TRACK YOUR PHONE.

STRANGER-   OH YES! YOU CAN'T TRACK ME AT ALL.

             GIVE ME A MILLION DOLLARS IF YOU

             WANT YOUR FACE TO BE SAFE.

PETUNIA –   OK! WHERE SHOULD I BRING IT?
             (With an idea in her mind)

STRANGER-   I'LL MESSAGE YOU MA'AM!

PETUNIA-   OK   *(hangs up the call).*

Petunia knew that the man's name certainly wasn't 'Silly.' She had the police track the call, but it wasn't working.

Let's see what happens next!

- Chapter Three-

Idea Implementing in Process

The stranger messaged his address to Petunia,

BIG RED BOX NEAR GOLDEN CITY HOUSE
CITY OF EUTOPIA

Petunia ventured to the location with a bag filled with thousands of papers. She kept the bag in the red box and pretended to then leave, but she didn't. She sneakily hid behind a gigantic pillar and waited for the man to arrive to nab him on the spot.

After thirty minutes of waiting, he arrived with the same mask on his face. Petunia ran towards the box and tried to capture him, but he was too strong. He lifted Petunia up and threw her down.

"Ouch!" muttered Petunia in pain. She chased him but in vain, he escaped.

Petunia proclaimed to take a troop of ten policemen with her to her next encounter with the stranger, as he was just too powerful.

The next day, she went to the police station and told them everything that had happened. She received another mysterious call from a different number. She picked it up and lo and behold, it was the criminal. She requested that the police listen to their conversation and attempt to track his phone in an endeavour to locate his whereabouts.

PETUNIA -   HELLO! GOT THE MONEY?

MAN   -   OH YEAH! I GOT PIECES OF PAPERS.
THANKS FOR THE LOVELY GIFT BUT IT ISN'T WHAT I NEEDED, YOU KNOW? HE FUMED, "WELL, YOU WILL GET YOUR GIFT SOON! GHOST FACE OR MAYBE A CLOWN. A CLOWN WOULD BE BETTER, I GUESS. CAN'T WAIT!! FAREWELL MS. PETUNIA."

PETUNIA -   (angrily hung up).

The police escorted her until the case was solved. Throughout the case, there were a few attempts to abduct her with no triumph. Her Karate, Kung-Fu and Hapkido skills helped her to a great extent to protect herself from any attacks. She was not going to be caught out again.

One day, when Petunia was roaming around a monument called Happy-go-Lucky tower, known for being shaped like a leaf, a person attempted to grab her in a car. That time, the policemen weren't with her as they had received an urgent task to complete. Petunia struggled to get herself free and thankfully, her Hapkido skills saved her.

Boldly, she followed the car, jumped in the front seat, hit the man driving, and put him inside the car's trunk and drove it to the police station. He was arrested and put into jail. Through the rush, Petunia didn't see the face of the person that she had captured as yet. She was too busy protecting herself.

She called upon the person in the hospital to help identify him. He was identified as being Iggy. Petunia screamed, "Yay, got one suspect."

She calmed herself down and asked him to write down whatever he knew, but he didn't give his full information.

After much interrogation, they managed to retrieve some pretty valuable intelligence,

> "I am Iggy Mathew. I work in a gang and my leader is Ace and his assistant is Theo. They are super crazy, crazier than me! They live here but in the negative side-North Eutopia. Please leave me now."

Manifestly, Petunia wouldn't leave him. She asked the police to secure him in jail. She was surprised to know that there was even a 'bad' part of Eutopia. She inquired about the area with the police.

The bad part of Eutopia was very small. It is actually called Jail-topia. It was the main location for crime-doers.

There are also some old houses and places that are abandoned or some say, haunted. The sun never rises clearly in that part of Eutopia, possibly due to the pollution in the area.

After receiving this information from the police, she rushed to North Eutopia.

Petunia noticed a tall jail building, some houses and a creepy, abandoned amusement park.

She could sense that something was off. She entered the jail building complex. It was very dirty and dusty. When she was walking, she noticed that the floor felt hollow beneath her and a hollow floor or wall to Petunia, always meant there was something down or behind there.

Petunia approached the staff and requested a hammer. She tried to break out. She started to break the floor to explore what was beneath, and promised to have it fixed later.

OMG! She had unearthed a whole room filled with skulls, ugly ghost figures and a lot of crazy things.

Inside, was a huge chair and the same type of mask which Petunia saw the stranger wearing on a small table. She picked it up and looked around for further clues. She found a picture of the man resembling a painting.

Petunia was very happy to find such a major clue. She observed the painting closely, but there was something bizarre about it. The eyes in the painting started to move! She took a deep breath…

- Chapter Four -

Let's Find Them

The painting started to move. It unfastened off the wall and started to walk. How was it possible?! It was in fact a man physically holding the painting with holes for eyes. Petunia apprehended and took him to the police station.

She called the person from the hospital once more to help identify this man. He said, "Petunia, this guy's name is Tool, and he had just escaped from the hospital this morning."

Petunia leered at him and asked him about the gang that he worked for. He kept quiet. She understood that he, surely was a part of the gang, so it was not going to be easy to get him to admit to anything.

She managed to eventually convince him and finally he claimed, "I joined a gang today itself. I got the invite from Theo, who is my leader, and his assistant, Ace."

Petunia was flabbergasted to hear this from the newly arrested suspect, as the statements of Tool and Iggy differed. Tool was taken back to the special hospital but still remanded in police custody.

Petunia's exploration continued. She returned to Jail-topia to examine the creepy amusement park, as it had a lot of buildings and sheds, in which either Ace or Theo or maybe both could be hiding. Two daring policemen, Dravid and Tim accompanied her for her protection.

The park was very dark. Petunia heard some scary noises all around. Suddenly, there was a loud sound.

THUD!

Oh no! Policeman Tim was lying on the ground, insensible with a wound on his leg.

Petunia thought, "Hmm…. An amusement park must have a first-aid box somewhere."

She saw an old building with a Red Cross mark. It was a clinic! Petunia and Dravid carried him there and there it was, the first aid kit. She locked all of the doors to avoid any problems with criminals.

She opened the first aid kit and was stunned to see that it only had one bandage and a unique golden box. She took the bandage and put it on Tim's leg.

Tim slowly woke up from his insensible state. Petunia asked him what had happened.

Tim's eyes started to glow green and his skin became yellowish. He stated, "Petunia! I have seen someone here. He had a machine in his hand. He shot an injection in my leg and it started to bleed. I don't know what happened to me after that. Let's find him. Quick!"

Just as Tim finished his statement, he astonishingly turned into a yellow devil right before their eyes. He could still do anything a person could, only his appearance changed.

The trio decided to solve the case then and there. Petunia knew that it had to be either Ace or Theo.

She wanted to check what was inside that golden box. It was locked!

She took a hairpin from her hair and opened the lock. She was startled to see a machine named Ghost Reverse.

She gave Tim the machine and he shot the liquid onto his injury. Glory, he no more looked like a ghost!

So…. that was the antidote for the ghost blaster machine!

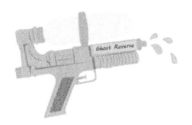

Petunia kept that machine with her. They noted, by the noises outside the room, that someone was trying to break the door of the clinic which she had locked to secure the room. She looked out of the window and saw a man just standing there.

He had a machine which had something written on it. Petunia took out a binoculars to read,

GHOST BLASTER MACHINE

Petunia, Dravid and Tim ran out of the clinic from another secret door. They took a turn, slowly walked to the main door and nabbed him. He was taken into the police van parked outside, where Petunia sat with him and questioned him as to what he was doing there.

He responded, "Why do you think I would tell you?" Petunia called upon an experienced psychologist to make him spill the truth. The psychologist had a great consultation and was able to acquire useful info from him…

"The liquid in the ghost blaster machine fell on his partner by mistake and he needed to come to the clinic because the antidote was kept there."

Petunia asked the man to tell him who he was and what his intention was. She assured him to give the antidote, if he showed honesty. He then decided to spill the beans. He said, "I am Theo. Ace is my brother, the one who called you and demanded one million dollars. He is the leader and I am his assistant. He is hiding in Shed no. 22 now."

Petunia's stranger enigma got resolved and she thanked the psychologist for his help.

- Chapter Five -

Shed No. 22

Petunia tied Theo up and secured the van so that he couldn't escape. She and the duo went in and examined the crappy map. The sheds were located towards the left. They looked for the number 22. There it was! They broke it open silently.

Inside was a bizarre and creepy clown. It was obviously Ace. He tried to run but the trio cornered and arrested him. They put him in the van and took him to the Eutopia Police Station.

Once they set foot there, Petunia gave him the antidote and tossed the pair into prison. The whole gang was now captured and in jail.

The police team thanked Petunia again for her phenomenal job. She urged the police to help them with rehabilitation programs.

Just then, the person from the special hospital arrived, looking worried. Petunia asked him what the matter was. He said, "I don't know how to say this, but... Tool has fled once more!"

Petunia was dismayed. She went to the special hospital to examine his room. It was neat and it seemed like everyone was being treated nicely too.

Petunia wandered along the street when she saw Tool running around wildly. Petunia greeted him and had a polite conversation with him. Petunia got to know from the conversation that the special hospital staff treated the people there abysmally.

They would hit and abuse them if they did something wrong and worse, they were not given adequate meals nor nutrition.

The other people who hadn't broke free suffered severe mental illnesses. They didn't understand anything.

Tool explained, "I was trying to catch a bus to run away from this city. My only problem was that I would get crazy at times but not always."

Petunia took Tool with her to the police station and elucidated the situation. She requested them to take immediate action upon the hospital to save the patients from further danger. The police took swift action and apprehended the hospital staff that were involved, and demanded the hospital management to hire qualified and professional new staff to treat people with kindness, affection and respect.

Petunia had not only helped the police catch some criminals but also she had improved the lives of people who were suffering at the hospital.

Petunia was awarded a memento for her bold and kind gesture. She was really exuberant.

She wrote two quotes from her vacation experience,

> Kindness always leads to good places for yourself or for others.

> A criminal always makes a small mistake in some way or another.

These quotes reached the Furors and they were published in a magazine along with Petunia's picture. The same happened in the city of Eutopia. They got renowned.

Petunia returned to the hotel room. Milly and Diana were taking a short nap. After an hour, they woke up and were thrilled to see Petunia after being away for many days. They ran to her and cuddled her.

Petunia proclaimed, "Now, we have fifteen days of holidays left. Let's go back to Furors and enjoy."

They cheered "yes" together.

- Chapter Six -

Back to Furors

Once they reached home, Diana was exhilarated to see Petunia's villa. She couldn't believe that Petunia owned a Lamborghini and a cute Pomeranian puppy named Daisy. Overjoyed, she played with the puppy for the whole day.

The next day, they went to mall and did a lot of shopping. They bought new clothes, toys, books, stationery and snacks. They even did some skydiving in the new skydiving centre, and visited one of the famous museums in the city.

They were engaged in various activities and they visited fascinating places in and around the city for the next fifteen days. The trio had a lot of fun and experiences to treasure.

Milly and Petunia were roomies or should I say, a mini family. They lived together and now, Diana was also a young, little family member.

Fifteen days had passed and Petunia returned to her office. Diana started going to one of the best schools in the city and Milly became busy spending time on her new animal research project.

Petunia Wolf

and

The Case

of the

Missing Princess

- Chapter One-

A New Case

Tring! Ring! Tring!

…Rang Petunia's phone. It was 5am in the morning. She, Milly and Diana were still fast asleep. Petunia woke up leisurely, rubbing her eyes and yawning. She stood up and answered the phone. It was a call from Officer Shawn.

PETUNIA - SALUTON OFICIRO SHAWN!

> *(Meaning 'Hello Officer Shawn' in Esperanto. Petunia only knows how to say that in Esperanto.)*

> WHAT IS THE MATTER? WHY HAVE YOU CALLED ME EARLY IN THE MORNING?

SHAWN - SALUTON PETUNIA!

> THERE IS A ROYAL FAMILY IN ARABIA WHOSE
> DAUGHTER, PRINCESS ZUBERI IS KIDNAPPED.
> THEY TRUST ONLY YOU TO SOLVE THIS CASE.
> PLEASE, WE NEED YOUR HELP. I WILL GET
> YOU A TICKET THERE.

PETUNIA- OK OFFICER! I AM READY FOR IT.

> I WILL COLLECT MY TICKET AT MY OFFICE.

SHAWN- THANK YOU PETUNIA! SEE YOU SOON.

(Call ended)

Petunia went back to sleep and woke up at her usual time. She told Milly and Diana about her trip to Arabia and that she was going alone, as it could be dangerous there for Diana and Milly.

She drove to her office. Officer Shawn was standing at the entrance with a slip of paper in his hands, waiting for her.

Petunia received her travel ticket and Officer Shawn provided her with available details on the new case.

Petunia drove to the airport in her Lamborghini and parked it in the long-term parking, then she boarded the plane.

It was a long flight. Almost twelve hours long. When she reached Arabia, the place was spectacular and the view was appealing. There were date palms, captivating sand dunes and camels wandering in the desert.

She went to the golden Royal Castle of Arabia and met the King, Asim and Queen, Celina pacing around worriedly.

Petunia communicated, "Hello your Royal Majesties! I am Petunia Wolf as you already know, and I am here to help find your daughter, her highness, Zuberi."

The King whined, "Oh Petunia! Please save my beloved daughter! I believe in you. Kindly stay here in the guest room until the case is solved."

Petunia assured them that she would solve the case and she thanked them for the luxurious room. She sat with King Asim and asked him a few questions.

"Who do you think could have done this? Do you suspect anyone?" Petunia asked.

The King replied, "Yes, I do suspect one person. Zuberi's uncle and Celina's brother, Asad. He lives in the Kingdom, but I still suspect him. He is always trying to get control of my Kingdom and he will go to any limits to do so.

I have received threatening calls from someone. They are demanding that I hand over my Kingdom in return for Zuberi.

"Great! Thank you. Can I please have a photo of Zuberi?"

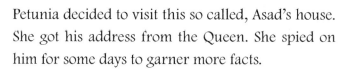

The King handed over a photograph of her, gloomily.

Looking at the picture, Petunia said, "Your daughter is very beautiful!"

"Yes, she is indeed!" The King agreed.

Petunia decided to visit this so called, Asad's house. She got his address from the Queen. She spied on him for some days to garner more facts.

- Chapter Two -

A Job Application

During her stay in the Kingdom, and while spying, Petunia overheard a conversation between Asad and another man. Asad was telling him to find a part-time maid, urgently.

Petunia dressed up as a maid, put a face prosthetic and a wig to look different. She applied for the job and of course, she was accepted.

She was told of all the chores that she was to do and was apprised not to enter one particular room in the house. Petunia thought that was questionable. She assumed that must be the room where he had locked up Zuberi.

Over the coming days, Petunia did what a good maid would do to gain Asad's trust by obeying and cleaning perfectly. Once she obtained his trust, Asad didn't have a watch on her any longer.

One day after her working hours, Petunia didn't leave. Instead, she waited for Asad to sleep. She snuck in and grabbed the key to the secret room, approached the secret room and opened the door, slowly. She was horrified to see, upon the wall, a board full of strategic plans on how to capture the Kingdom.

But Zuberi was nowhere to be spotted. She took pictures and showed it to the King and his loyal and royal team the next day. They were petrified by seeing that.

Petunia went back to her room and examined the pictures closely. She observed them in detail to find every possible clue. She saw a tiny photo of Princess Zuberi with a thick thread leading to another picture of an old, dirty and mossy barn. She thought that must be it, the place she was looking for! Where the Princess would be kept.

The next morning when she went to Asad's house, he seemed very angry. He yelled at her, "How dare you! I trusted you. How did you not listen to me? Huh!?"

He was about to belabour her but then Petunia exhibited her incredible martial art skills, disabled his response and took him to the palace jail. He was interrogated by her but he didn't respond to any of the questions. Petunia left him in jail while she went off in search for Princess Zuberi.

She asked the King and Queen if they knew where the barn was. Unfortunately, they too didn't have the faintest idea for the Kingdom and surrounding village was vast. She went out of the castle grounds and advanced towards a nearby village in search of the barn.

She went to all twenty houses in the village enquiring about it. At last, one man disclosed, "The barn is ten miles from here. There is a sign board with the name, 'Moss Barn.' That is where you'll find it."`

Petunia thanked him in Arabic, 'Shukran' and hit the road. She arrived there at warp speed and broke open the barn with a hammer that she had packed in her bag.

Inside, she just found some dirty sheets of paper and ancient vases. She checked the sheets and found a letter.

Upon the letter was written,

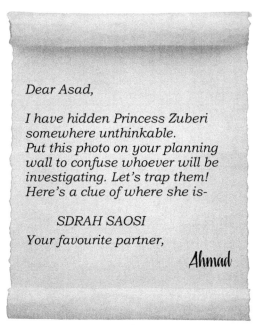

Dear Asad,

*I have hidden Princess Zuberi
somewhere unthinkable.
Put this photo on your planning
wall to confuse whoever will be
investigating. Let's trap them!
Here's a clue of where she is-*

   SDRAH SAOSI
Your favourite partner,

Ahmad

Petunia knew now that she was being trapped by
Asad and Ahmad. She un-jumbled the second word
which was 'OASIS' but the first one was unclear to
her.

She researched via the internet about some oases in
Arabia and at last found the name that seemed
correct-   DHASR OASIS

- Chapter Three -

Dhasr Oasis

She traced the location and decided to go there with armour on her body and a razor-sharp sword, as Ahmad may have planned a deadly attack. She needed to be prepared.

She arrived there by taxi, well prepared with her package. Once she stepped on the hot sand near the oasis, people holding weapons emerged from all around. Petunia was right about the deadly attack. She bravely faced all of them with her mighty sword. Almost all of them were injured at the end.

Petunia went closer and closer to the oasis. Inside, the oasis, Petunia saw something strange. She took a rope from her bag and dived deep into the oasis by tying it to a strong big Ghaf tree.

The oasis was indeed very deep. Unexpectedly, Petunia saw a small villa underwater made of cement which was further coated with tar paper, a waterproof material.

Petunia slipped in and saw a man in Arabic attire. He had his phone on speaker mode and was speaking to someone. Petunia assumed that he was Ahmad. Her intelligence was correct. The man had just taken his name.

She overheard their whole conversation and got to know the actual location of where Zuberi was hidden,

"Old Village Mart"

The call ended and Ahmad came near the door to see outside, as he sensed something unusual. Petunia swam swiftly and went to the back door to hide.

Ahmad came to the back door and Petunia swam to the front door. Ahmad had seen her leg, but phew! He considered that she had been diving for pearls as that oasis was famous for its unique pearls.

- Chapter Four -

Finding Zuberi

Petunia quickly came out of the oasis. She booked a taxi and went to Old Village Mart which was at a really far distance from there, about two hundred miles away. It was a three-hour long drive.

Once she arrived there, she needed to find some food first, as she was starving. She had falafels as a starter, Manakeesh as the main course and Lokma as dessert in the local popular restaurant, Arabian Kitchen.

"Yum, Yum!" savoured Petunia.

Petunia paid the bill and took a tour of the town. She visited all of the houses and places except for just one, a luxurious building called Burj Al-Hadiqa, meaning Garden Tower.

She showed her fake ID which she had taken from another woman and entered the building. Nobody suspected her.

Name-Emily Smith
Age-23
Working area- Garden
Tower, Arabia

She crept into the elevator and pressed all the buttons. One by one, the door opened and closed until all thirty floors were complete.

Petunia noticed a small staircase on the thirtieth floor. She climbed up the staircase, and saw a mini room. The door was open and Petunia entered. There she heard a girl's murmur! She listened closely and ran in the direction of the sound.

She saw a man wearing a mask running with a little girl whose hands and legs were tied with rope, and her mouth was masked. Petunia saw her face. It was indeed Princess Zuberi! She ran swiftly behind the man and caught him after what seemed like a mini marathon.

Petunia started to hit the man. Then, she dragged him to the taxi. She shoved him into the vehicle's trunk.

She freed Princess Zuberi and asked if she was okay and if she needed or wanted anything.

She said, "I am okay and I don't want anything. I just want to see my parents. Anyway, who are you? Thank you for saving me. It's Asad and his men who kidnapped me to take over daddy's Kingdom."

Petunia said, "Relax, I am taking you to your parents now. I am Petunia Wolf. You might have heard about me. Asad is already in the jail and soon his partner, Ahmad will also be there, and so will their team."

Princess Zuberi was extremely happy to hear this and affirmed that she had heard Petunia's name said throughout the Kingdom. She was eager to meet her parents.

- Chapter Five -

To the Kingdom!

Petunia reached the palace and dragged the man with the mask to the King and Queen. Zuberi ran to her parents with excitement. Her parents cried tears of joy and hugged her. They expressed their gratitude to Petunia.

She imparted, "The case is not fully solved. Let's see who the actual criminal is, shall we, your majesties?"

The royal parents chorused yes. Petunia pulled the mask off the culprit's face. The King was outraged upon seeing his face. The queen was also appalled.

Petunia rushed to the King and Queen and asked who he was.

The King felt downhearted and said, "This is my most trusted minister, Alakam. You were working with that Asad! I should have realized. Guards! Come and arrest him and keep him in jail for the rest of his life."

The Queen also nodded in agreement. Petunia was shocked. The guards took him away. The King promised Petunia that their guards would arrest Ahmad and the rest of the troop and that all will be punished for their deeds.

She expressed, "I trust you majesties and I am glad to see Zuberi back in the Kingdom."

The royals thanked her profusely once more. Petunia responded merrily, "You are always welcome, your highnesses! I think I should leave now as my mission is over."

The King and Queen insisted on Petunia staying for another day and she agreed.

- Chapter Six -

Surprise!

Petunia woke up the next morning, got ready and came down to greet the King and Queen. It was dark there in the large dining room.

Aghast, she gingerly moved forward. In a trice, lights adorned the room and Officer Shawn, Milly, King Asim, Queen Celina, Princess Zuberi, Diana and Petunia's whole team from Furors came out of nowhere. They all screamed, "Happy Birthday Petunia!!!"

Petunia herself, had forgotten that it was her birthday. She was enchanted to see the arrangements. There was a huge cake on the table. She was overwhelmed with joy!

They all had a group hug and then, Petunia started to cut the cake when the King stopped her. He gave her a hammer and told her to smash the cake instead.

She smashed her cake with the two little girls, Diana and Zuberi. It was a piñata cake! They all clapped and couldn't wait to taste it.

A royal chef came into the room and distributed the cake to all of the guests and of course, Petunia received the largest slice!

The cake tasted delicious and the flavour was unique. She asked the Queen which flavour it was. She said that it was a new flavour. A special Arab flavour called Kunafa Choco-Cheese Cake.

All of them relished it! Milly sat with her and recounted how the surprise party was all the King's idea.

Petunia felt honoured and blessed. She went to the King, bowed and thanked him. The King smiled and asserted, "Petunia, you deserve it! You have saved my daughter from that maniac, Asad. Thank you so, so much! We will never forget this in our lives."

Petunia thanked him once more. It was a wonderful and the most memorable day for Petunia! She received many gifts. This was, for sure, her best birthday party ever and she was very gleeful!

The End.

Dear Avid readers,

Thank you for reading
this Jim-dandy book. I
hope that you will join
me in my next bodacious
adventure coming soon
so adieu till then!

About the Author

Afsheen Sheikh

The Author of this book is Afsheen Sheikh, a ten-year old girl from India, living in Abu Dhabi, UAE. She is cordial, innovative and zestful who loves reading the facts of various things around the world.

At her leisure, she loves to draw, colour, paint and sketch. She invests her imagination in writing stories and poems. She has a sweet tooth and is acquiring baking as a new hobby.

She desires to be happy and successful in her life. She dreams to see this world as the best place to live in for all and wishes to contribute her part in shaping so.

A NOTE FROM THE AUTHOR
I WISH TO SEE YOU SOON IN
PETUNIA'S NEXT ADVENTURE-
PETUNIA WOLF,
THE CASE-CRACKER
BOOK-2

FOLLOW AFSHEEN'S WRITING JOURNEY HERE...

www.youngauthoracademy.com/afsheen-sheikh

Printed in Great Britain
by Amazon

64753718R00058